THE FIXIT MAN

STORY BY **IRMA WILDE**
PICTURES BY **GEORGE WILDE**

G+D VINTAGE

Once there was a happy little man named
Mr. Aloysius Christopher James Jinks.

But that was such a very long name, and
he was such a little man, that everyone called
him Jimmy Jinks for short.

Jimmy Jinks was a very happy man and he loved his work. He worked hard every day, for Jimmy Jinks was a handyman—a Mr. Fixit who mended all sorts of things.

He could fix broken sewing machines. He could put new handles on old umbrellas. And he could sharpen lawn mowers and ice skates and scissors.

Jimmy Jinks used many different tools
to help him with his work. He had big pliers
and little pliers, a little grindstone, lots of
screwdrivers and hammers, and all sorts of
wires and nails. Jimmy Jinks kept all these
tools in a little wagon that his horse pulled
around the streets.

Every morning folks heard his bell and his
cheery little song:

"Have you umbrellas to mend, or skates to grind?
Please bring them all to Jimmy Jinks,
And he'll make them look just fine."

Everyone would scurry about gathering up
their broken lawn mowers, dull skates, and
torn umbrellas. They would bring them out to
Jimmy Jinks so that he could make them like
new again.

Dear, dear! said Jimmy Jinks to himself one day. There must be a lot of people in the world trying to do their work with old and broken tools. And how very hard that must be. I think I'll travel around a little.

And he started out that very day.

First he came to a big farmhouse. He rang
his bell and sang:

"I'm Jimmy Jinks, the Fixit Man,

I fix and patch as fast as I can."

The farmer brought out a broken plow,

and Jimmy Jinks put a nice new handle on it.

The farmer's wife called him into the house to
fix her sewing machine. She was so happy to have
her sewing machine working again that she gave
Jimmy Jinks a piece of cherry pie for his lunch!

The farmer's son, who was watching Jimmy
Jinks, decided he'd be a Fixit Man, too, when
he grew up.

Jimmy Jinks traveled on to the seashore.

All the fishermen were very sad. Their nets had big holes in them, and they couldn't catch any fish!

Jimmy Jinks rang his bell and sang:

"I'll mend your nets as quick as you wish,

And abracadabra, you'll catch lots of fish!"

Jimmy Jinks went to work and the fishermen were delighted with their mended nets. They got into their boats and sailed off to catch their fish.

Jimmy Jinks traveled on again. He climbed
up into the mountains. And there he found
a very unhappy woodsman. The woodsman
was trying to cut down a big tree with an ax
so dull that it wouldn't cut even a little stick.

"Dear, dear, this will never do," said Jimmy
Jinks. So he rang his bell and sang:
"I'll sharpen your ax and make it strong,
And you'll cut down that tree before very long."

"Hurray!" cried the woodsman. Sure enough, when Jimmy Jinks had sharpened the ax, the woodsman cut the tree right down.

"Good-bye," called Jimmy Jinks, and he traveled on his way again.

Jimmy Jinks is still riding around, fixing sewing machines and umbrellas, and sharpening lawn mowers and ice skates and scissors.

Jimmy Jinks, the Fixit Man, has made many people happy—and they are always glad to hear his bell and his cheery little song.